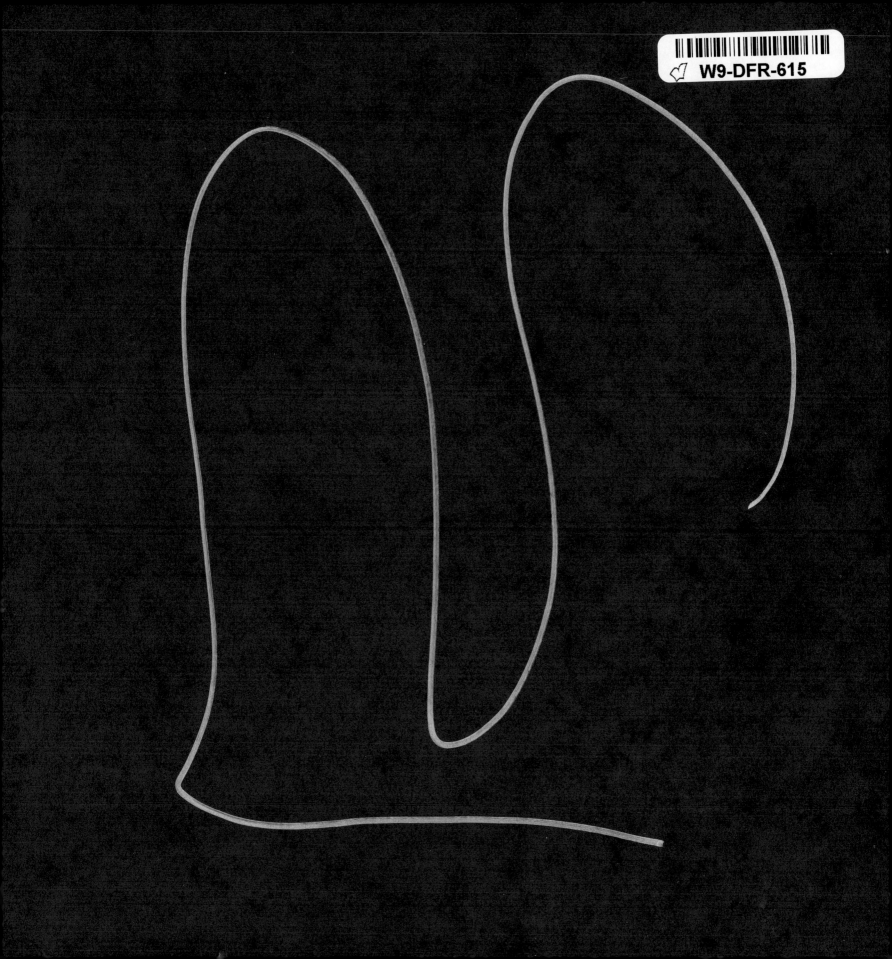

BROTHER RABBIT

A CAMBODIAN TALE

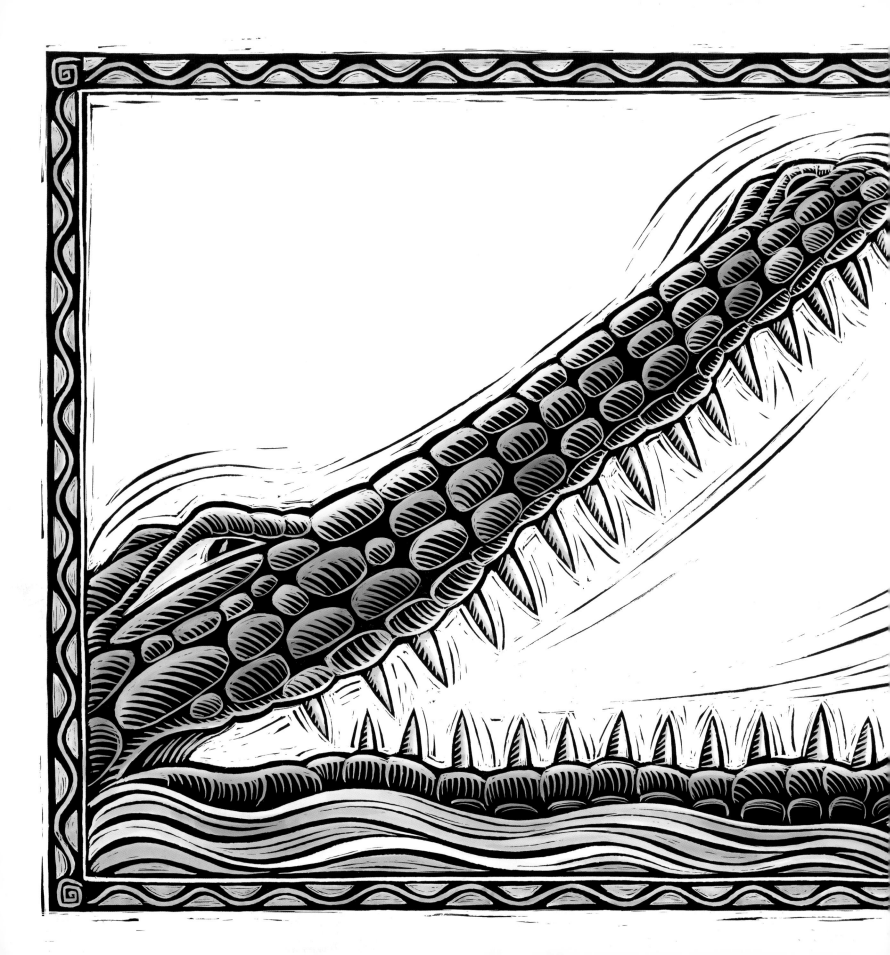

BROTHER RABBIT

A CAMBODIAN TALE

BY MINFONG HO & SAPHAN ROS

ILLUSTRATED BY JENNIFER HEWITSON

LOTHROP, LEE & SHEPARD BOOKS
NEW YORK

I would like to dedicate this book to the memory of those of my family
who were killed during the Pol Pot regime.
This story is also for my own children—Rithy, Chhorvy, Linda, and Duong—
from whom I was separated in 1978 during the war,
as well as for little Vimol and Tepvaddei,
who I hope will read this in school someday.

—SR

for Cambodian children and their friends everywhere

—MH

to Grandma Hewitson and her dreams, in loving memory

—JH

The illustrations in this book were done in watercolor paints and ink. The display type was set in Roxy. The text was set in Charlotte Sans.
Printed and bound by South China Printing Company. Production supervised by Linda Palladino. Designed by Charlotte Hommey.
Text copyright © 1997 by Minfong Ho and Saphan Ros
Illustrations copyright © 1997 by Jennifer Hewitson
Printed in Hong Kong.
First Edition   1 2 3 4 5 6 7 8 9 10
Library of Congress Cataloging in Publication Data
Ho, Minfong. Brother Rabbit / by Minfong Ho and Saphan Ros; illustrated by Jennifer Hewitson.
p.   cm. Summary: A crocodile, two elephants, and an old woman are no match for a mischievous rabbit.
ISBN 0-688-12552-2. — ISBN 0-688-12553-0 (lib. bdg.) [1. Folklore—Cambodia. 2. Rabbits—Folklore.] I. Ros, Saphan.
II. Hewitson, Jennifer, ill. III. Title. PZ8.1.H6674Br 1994
398.24'529322—dc20 [E] 92-38206 CIP AC

A NOTE ABOUT THIS STORY

The diversity of Cambodia's folktales reflects the country's long and rich history, which dates back almost two thousand years to the first century AD, when its royal courts adopted an alphabet and a legal code. Through the generations, the people of Cambodia have handed down countless stories about little animals and wild monsters, cruel kings and clever peasants, sailing ships and magic potions.

Traditionally, folktales were told by grandparents to village children in the cool of the evening. More elaborate presentations took the form of folk plays known as *yikay.* These were performed by small theatrical troupes that traveled from one village to another. Dancers pantomimed the action as a narrator sang the story to the accompaniment of drums or the two-stringed Khmer violin. Although the main story line remained traditional, the lively narrators and actors often improvised, adding details of local interest, much to the delight of their audiences.

One of the recurring themes in Cambodian folktales is that of a small but quick-witted animal or person getting the better of someone stronger and meaner but not as bright. In Cambodian society, farmers and villagers saw themselves as small and weak compared to the powerful landlords, soldiers, and kings above them, and they reveled in stories in which the tables were turned and the weak came out on top.

Nationally, too, Cambodia has often seen itself as the weaker nation among stronger, more aggressive neighbors. Although from the ninth to the thirteenth centuries the Khmer Empire extended far into the kingdoms of present-day Thailand, Laos, and Vietnam, for the last seven hundred years Cambodia saw its powers decline as its neighbors grew stronger. More recently, during the years of the Vietnam War, the United States and the Soviet Union used Cambodia as a pawn in their own conflicts, resulting in terrible suffering for the Cambodians. The bombing of Cambodia by the United States in the late 1960s and early 1970s was followed by the despotic rule of the Khmer Rouge from 1975 to 1979. It is only in recent years that a fragile peace has been established.

Against this background, the folktale of *Brother Rabbit* is especially apt. In it a small rabbit outwits a sharp-fanged crocodile. Time and again, just as Brother Rabbit is about to be devoured by the crocodile, he saves himself by being quick-witted and clever. And he manages to stay cheerful through it all.

Like Brother Rabbit, the Cambodian people have remained irrepressible in the face of constant warfare, ready to rebuild their lives again through their quick wits and their resilience.

Minfong Ho
Saphan Ros
1996

BROTHER RABBIT was hopping along early one morning when he noticed a patch of tender rice seedlings just planted in the field across the river. Now, rabbits love to eat rice seedlings, and Brother Rabbit was no exception. He decided to cross the river and sneak into the field for a feast.

But how could he cross the river?
As he stood on the riverbank pondering this, a crocodile swam along.
What luck! Brother Rabbit thought. *I bet I can get this crocodile to give me a ride across.*

So he called out, "Oh, what a strong and beautiful creature you are! Could you please swim a little closer so I can get a better look at you?"

Flattered, the crocodile swam over to the rabbit and crawled up the muddy bank.

"But your skin!" Brother Rabbit exclaimed then, pretending to be shocked. "Why is it so rough and ugly?"

"I think it's a disease called ringworm," the crocodile answered.

"I can get rid of it for you," said Brother Rabbit, "if you just ferry me across the river."

Happy to hear this good news, the crocodile smiled toothily at Brother Rabbit. "Get on," he said. "If you can cure me of my rough skin, I'll be glad to give you a ride."

So the rabbit got on, but not before he had carefully put a lotus leaf on top
of the crocodile's head so he wouldn't have to sit on the scaly skin.
"Why are you putting a leaf on my head?" the crocodile asked.

"Because I respect you too much to touch you on the head," the rabbit lied.

Satisfied, the crocodile swam across the river with the rabbit sitting on his head.

When they reached the other bank, Brother Rabbit jumped off and started to run away.

"Wait!" the crocodile shouted. "What about my rough skin?"

"Idiot," said the rabbit. "You got that from your parents and grandparents! There's nothing *I* can do about it." And laughing, he hopped off to the field of seedlings.

Just you wait, the crocodile thought angrily as he watched Brother Rabbit disappear. *I'll teach you to make fun of me! The next time I see you, I'll pretend to be a log, and I'll bite you in half when you step on me.*

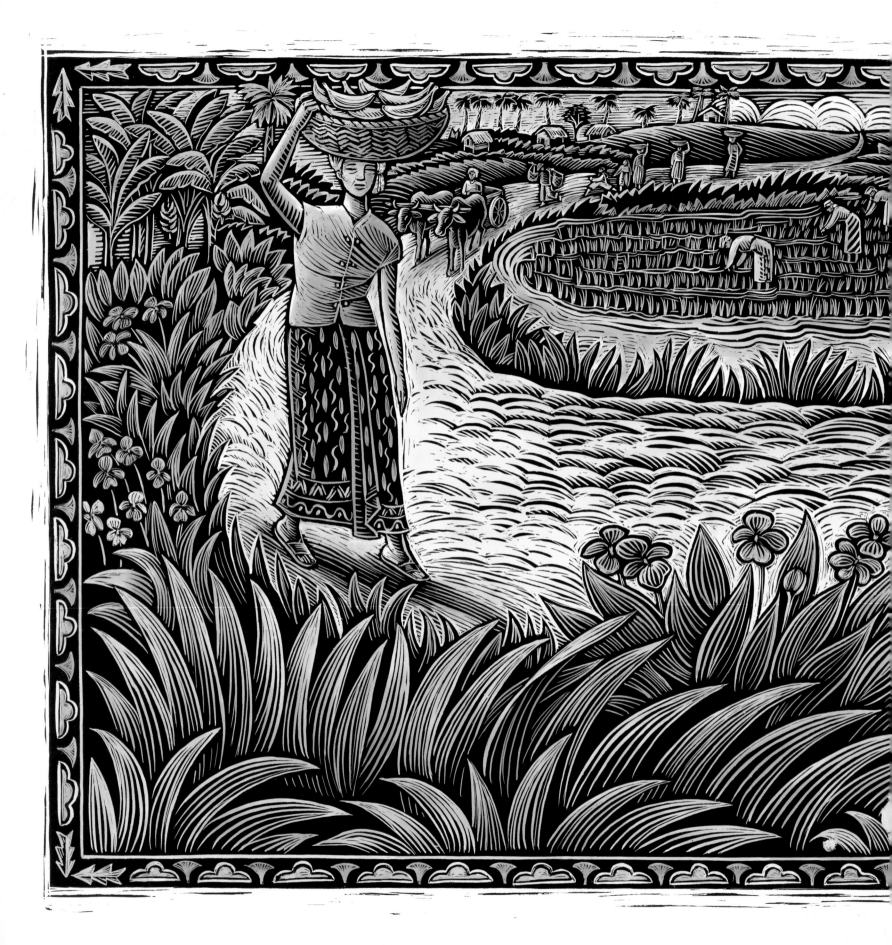

After Brother Rabbit had eaten his fill of seedlings, he hopped along the fields. In the distance he saw a woman on her way to market. On her head was a basket of bananas. How sweet and ripe those bananas looked.

Brother Rabbit was determined to get some for himself, so he crept up the road and lay there, very still. When the woman came along, she thought the rabbit was dead.

"What a lucky day!" she exclaimed. "I can have rabbit curry for dinner." And so saying, she picked up the limp rabbit and tossed him into her basket.

Of course, as soon as he was inside the basket, Brother Rabbit began to eat the bananas. By the time the woman arrived at the market, he had finished every one. When she lowered the basket from her head, he jumped out and ran away, leaving only a pile of banana peels behind him.

It was high noon when Brother Rabbit returned to the river. He stood on the riverbank, wondering how he was going to get back home. Just then something long and brown floated by him.

"Now I wonder," said Brother Rabbit, "is that a log or a crocodile floating by?" He raised his voice. "If it's a log, it should float upstream. But if it's a crocodile, it should float downstream."

The crocodile—for that was indeed who it was—heard the rabbit.

Well, he thought, *since I am pretending to be a log, I had better do what he says and float upstream.* So, very carefully, paddling his feet underwater, he started to swim upstream.

When Brother Rabbit saw the "log" floating against the current, he burst out laughing. "So it is you after all, Mr. Crocodile!" he shouted. "You can't fool me!"

The crocodile was furious. He thrashed around, trying to bite Brother Rabbit, but the rabbit just skipped gaily back to the safety of the rice fields.

Next time, the crocodile vowed silently, *I'll pretend to be dead, and when he gets close enough, I'll gulp him right down!*

After hopping along in the hot sun for a while, Brother Rabbit felt tired, so he sat down on a tree stump next to a pond. But as he rested, the sun melted the resin on the stump, gluing his tail onto the wood. When Brother Rabbit tried to jump off, he was stuck fast to the stump.

Just then a baby elephant came to drink from the pond.
"Hey, stop that!" Brother Rabbit shouted. "You can't drink my water!"
Startled, the baby elephant ran to tell his mother.

Soon the mother elephant came lumbering down to the pond. "Why can't my son drink that pond water?" she demanded.

"Because the gods have ordered me to guard it against big, stupid animals like the two of you," Brother Rabbit retorted.

Furious, the mother elephant twisted her trunk around the rabbit's neck,
ripping him free from the sticky tree stump, and flung him away.
    "Thanks for setting me free!" the rabbit yelled cheerfully as he ran off.

It was already twilight, and Brother Rabbit was eager to get back to his home across the river. So back to the riverbank he went, and there he came across the crocodile again. This time, of course, he was playing dead. His huge jaws were stretched open, wide and stiff.

Brother Rabbit approached the crocodile cautiously and looked into the
gaping jaws. "Oh, what smooth, sharp fangs," he said.
    The crocodile didn't stir.

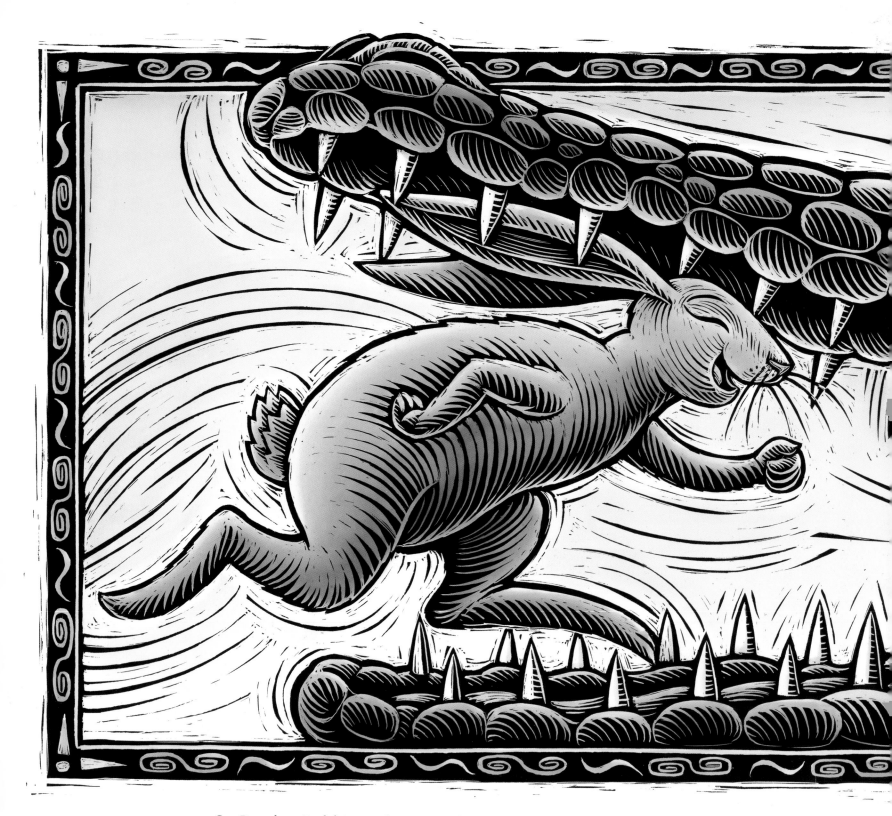

So Brother Rabbit took a step closer and touched the crocodile's teeth. "I'll pry out the big fangs to make a new handle for my pocketknife," he said. "And I'll use the small fangs to make a new handle for my wife's kitchen knife." Still the crocodile didn't move.

Sure now that the crocodile was really dead, Brother Rabbit became bold and careless. He walked right into the gaping jaws. And at that moment, the crocodile snapped his mouth shut and gulped Brother Rabbit right down!

But if Brother Rabbit was frightened, he didn't show it. Instead, he ran deeper and deeper into the crocodile's belly. "Isn't this wonderful!" he shouted. "I've always wanted to eat crocodile guts. Now that I'm in his belly, I can eat all his insides!" Then he thumped his feet against the walls of the crocodile's belly for sound effects.

The poor crocodile was so terrified that he trembled. "Brother Rabbit, please get out," he begged. "Don't eat up my insides!"

"Promise that you'll never try to trick me again," said Brother Rabbit, "and I might have pity on you."

The crocodile promised.

"And you might as well give me a ride back across the river," Brother Rabbit added, "*if* I come out."

"Oh, I will, I will," said the crocodile.

"All right, then. Open your mouth wide," said the rabbit, "and hurry up. It's getting a little stuffy in here."

The crocodile was only too glad to open his jaws. Taking his time, Brother Rabbit strolled out into the open air.

Together they recrossed the river just as daylight was fading, and Brother Rabbit reached home tired but happy with his day's adventures. As for the crocodile, he never tried to trick Brother Rabbit again.